FOSSIL MAZE

Fly
ISLAND

CHOPPY SEAS

POINTY ROCKS

WHIRLPOOL

Roo
ISLAND

CALM SEAS

Starfish

MYSTERY ISLAND

Roo

The Roaring Dinosaur
Best Playday Ever!

For Mandy, for playing
– DB

For Timothy Stimpson
– MS

SIMON AND SCHUSTER
First published in Great Britain in 2016 by Simon and Schuster UK Ltd
1st Floor, 222 Gray's Inn Road, London WC1X 8HB

A CBS Company

Text copyright © 2016 David Bedford

Illustrations copyright © 2016 Mandy Stanley

The right of David Bedford and Mandy Stanley to be identified as the author
and illustrator of this work has been asserted by them in accordance with
the Copyright, Designs and Patents Act, 1988
All rights reserved, including the right of reproduction in
whole or in part in any form
A CIP catalogue record for this book is available from
the British Library upon request

ISBN: 978-1-4711-4503-2 (HB)
ISBN: 978-1-4711-4504-9 (PB)
ISBN: 978-1-4711-4505-6 (eBook)
Printed in China
2 4 6 8 10 9 7 5 3 1

Roo

The Roaring Dinosaur
Best Playday Ever!

David Bedford & Mandy Stanley

Roo the Roaring Dinosaur
lived in a little dinosaur house on
a little dinosaur island.

It was
Roo's home!

Every morning Roo
hopped out to play.

Today Roo
decided to go . . .

that way!

SEA

Off he sped
on his scooter.

Wheee!

He **splished** and **splashed**
along the hot, sandy beach.

Then Roo dug deep holes
and piled up the sand to make . . .

'Sand Roo!'
said Roo.

Just as he finished . . .

. . . he heard rustling
in the trees.

Somebody
was there!

'Roo hide!'
he said.

'Boo!' said Roo, bravely.

'Hello!' said the new creature, who was big, fluffy and very friendly.

'I'm Erik. I'm so glad I found your island, Roo.

This map showed me the way.'

'Can I sit down?' said Erik.
And he sat on the Sand Roo!

'Oooops,'

said Erik.

Erik Island

'Sorry. I'm always doing things like that.'

Erik didn't mean to be clumsy, so Roo took him along the beach, splishing and splashing.

'Ooops!'
said Erik.

They **jumped** through a sparkling waterfall.

'Ooops!' said Erik.

Roo decided to take Erik somewhere a little less wet.

Roo showed Erik how to swing round and round a tree.

'Ooops!'
said Erik.

At last they climbed the steep steps to the top of the old volcano.

'Wow,' said Erik. 'I can see all of your island from here.'

When Roo looked too, he saw something he had never seen before.

'That's my ice ship,'
said Erik, proudly.

Then he gasped.

'OH NO!
It's melting!'

Roo and Erik scrambled
down to the seashore.

Roo jumped into
his little boat . . .

. . . and soon towed the
ice ship away from the
hot beach and out to sea.

But now there was almost
nothing left of the ice ship!

Erik looked very worried.
'Can I get in with you,
Roo?' he said.

Roo wasn't sure if he wanted Erik in his boat.
Erik was always breaking things.
He might break Roo's little boat, too.

'Please!' called Erik from
his little bit of ice.

'I'll be very
careful! I promise!'

So Roo made a
brave decision.

'Erik, jump!' he said,

Then . . .

'ROOOOO!' roared Roo in surprise.

Erik rowed and rowed and **rowed**. Roo's little boat had never gone so fast!

And in hardly any
time at all . . .

Erik had
rowed **home!**

'Stay for tea,'
said Erik.

'I bet you've
never played in
the snow before.'

Roo liked snow.
He dug deep holes
and made . . .

'Snow Erik!'

said Roo.

Then they sat together and shared
sips of steaming hot chocolate, and watched
bright night colours swirling and dancing
and bursting in the sky.

But when Erik went to make more hot
chocolate. Roo began to shiver.

Erik's island was far too
cold for a little dinosaur.

It was time for Roo
to go home.

'Here,' said Erik. 'Take the map, it'll help you to . . .

Oh no!
I've ripped it
in two!'

'Ooops!' said Roo.
Erik and Roo giggled
and giggled.

Roo rowed back across the
big waves. He thought of Erik's
strong paws pulling on the oars.

And he rowed and rowed
and **rowed**, and in hardly
any time at all . . .

Roo was **home!**

'Roooo!'

'Roooo!' he roared as
he raced along on his scooter.

'Hoooo!' he sang
as he sprang into his little
dinosaur house,
and . . .

'Roo-hoo!' he smiled, thinking about his funny new friend and the **best playday ever.**

Erik Island

The End